Susan Jeschke

Mia, Grandma and the Genie

Holt, Rinehart and Winston • New York

To Miriam Chaikin

Library of Congress Cataloging in Publication Data

Jeschke, Susan.
   Mia, Grandma and the Genie

   SUMMARY: Mia comes to understand her grandmother's
friendship with her household items, nature, and the
ugly genie in the earthenware jar.
   [1. Grandmothers–Fiction.   2. Magic–Fiction]
I. Title.
PZ7.J553Mi   [E]   77-5699
ISBN 0-03-028586-0

It was nearly dawn. The sounds coming from the next room woke
Mia. She got up and listened. Grandma was shuffling about,
talking to her friends—the table, the chairs, the frying pan, and
the teapot—and to her special friend, the genie.
The genie lived in a covered jar on the mantel. And every night
Mia heard Grandma and the genie laughing and talking together.
Mia had never seen the genie. Whenever she tried to catch
a glimpse of him, all she saw was Grandma, talking and laughing
to herself.

"Get out of bed. It's here," Grandma said. "Let's welcome the sun."

Grandma hugged Mia, threw a shawl around her, and bustled her off to the next room where they both stood facing the east window. As the sun began to fill the small room, everything began to glow—the table, the chairs, the frying pan, the teapot, the genie jar. "Ummm, thank you for coming today," Grandma said. Mia yawned.

"If you don't make it feel welcome, it won't come," said Grandma.

"I'm hungry," Mia said.

As Mia turned a cartwheel to the table, the shawl fell off and she knocked over a chair. Grandma picked them up.

"Mia, apologize!" Grandma said.
"Oh, Grandma, I'm not going to apologize to a scratchy old shawl or a chair," Mia said.
"It was an accident. She didn't mean it," Grandma said to the shawl and chair.

Grandma went to the stove, and the frying pan sizzled, and the room filled with delicious smells.
Soon, three golden pancakes were placed in front of Mia.
Grandma thanked the pan.
Then she cleaned it and rubbed it until it shone.
"Ummm," said Mia.
As she reached for the syrup, she knocked over her tea.

Quickly, Grandma mopped up the table.
"Apologize!" she said.
"I'm not talking to a table!" Mia answered.
Grandma turned to the table. "She really didn't mean it,"
she said. She looked at Mia. "They are all your good friends.
You must be more thankful for the good they do you."

Mia ate breakfast, then dusted. Grandma had warned her
to take special care of the genie jar. Today, however,
Mia opened the genie jar and threw a candy wrapper inside
to see what would happen.

As though she had eyes in the back of her head, Grandma flew to
the jar, threw out the wrapper, then slapped Mia.
"You are being disrespectful!" Grandma said.
"For generations he has been a friend to our family."
"I just wanted to see if he was there."
"He's there. You'll see him when you need him."
Mia apologized for Grandma's sake.
Grandma sighed.
As the days wore on, Mia noticed that Grandma sighed more
and more and complained of aches.

One day, a doctor came and said Grandma should go to the hospital for a while. Mia helped Grandma pack a small suitcase.
There was a knock on the door, and two men came in with a stretcher.
"Take care of yourself— and everyone," Grandma said.

With tears in her eyes, Mia watched the ambulance drive off.

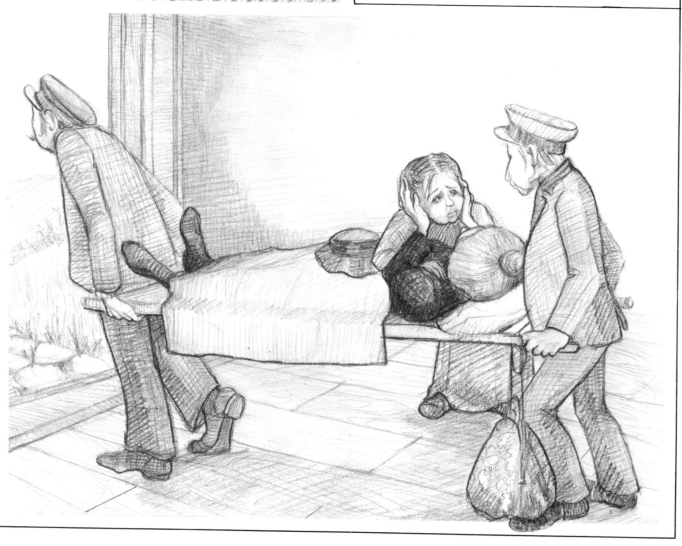

The little house seemed grey without Grandma.
Good smells no longer came from the kitchen.
The frying pan seemed to lose its luster.
Dust settled on the table and chairs.
Even the sun seemed to stop shining.
It was lonely without Grandma.
After some days, Mia decided to go to the hospital to see Grandma.

"What can I bring to cheer her up?"
she wondered, looking around
the room.
The table and chairs were too big
to carry. The frying pan and teapot
wouldn't be good without the stove.
"The genie jar!" she thought, and
tucked it under her arm.

It was a long way to the hospital.

At night, Mia lay down under a tree.
She covered herself with the shawl.
A terrible loneliness seized her.
Then she remembered Grandma's
companion.

She lifted the lid—
and out came the genie.

At first, Mia was terrified.
But the genie was very kind,
and soon she was no longer lonely.
She laughed and talked the
night away with the genie.

When it grew light, the genie
slipped back into the jar.
Mia folded the shawl
and continued on her way.

Mia ate some berries she found along the road. As she sat on a rock eating them, she thought of the comfortable chair— and the good things that used to come from Grandma's frying pan. She continued on her way.

As dusk was approaching, Mia noticed a campfire.

She drew closer. There was Grandma's table! And two strange men, sitting in Grandma's chairs! One was banging Grandma's pan on the ground, cursing it for having burnt his food.

"Too bad there was nothing valuable in that house," said the other man. But if we can't sell this junk, we can always use it for firewood." He took out a knife and seemed about to plunge it into the table.

"Stop!" Mia screamed. The men jumped up.
"Those are my grandmother's!" she said.
The men laughed. "What's that?" asked one, looking at the jar.
"Nothing," Mia said, hugging the jar to herself.

"Give it here!" said the man with the knife. Mia shook her head NO— and backed away.
The men went after her.

Mia ducked under the table.
The man with the knife tripped
on the chair—
and his knife sailed into the air—
and landed in the teapot.
The other man's foot got stuck
in the frying pan—and he fell.

Mia tried to escape—
but it was too late. She was thrown
to the ground, and the jar was pulled
from her hands.

The men ran for their lives.

Mia put the pan and teapot on the table and sat down.
"Thank you all," she said. She ate the food the robbers
had left behind.
Mia couldn't remember when it felt so good to sit on
the chair or eat at the table.

Again she laughed and talked late into the night with the genie, until she fell asleep.

Early the next morning,
Mia arrived at the hospital.

She found Grandma standing and
looking out of the window.
A smile spread across Grandma's face
when she saw Mia and the genie jar.
"What a surprise. The very day
the doctor said I could go home!"
Grandma said.

The sun came up as they were
leaving the hospital.
"Thank you for coming today, sun,"
Mia said.
Grandma took Mia's hand, and
together they set off for home.

About the Author

Susan Jeschke was born in Cleveland, Ohio, and presently
lives in Brooklyn, New York. She attended classes
at the School of Visual Arts and the Brooklyn Museum School,
studying printmaking, sculpture, and illustration.
    She is the author-artist of *Firerose*, an ALA Notable Book
for 1974, *Sidney, The Devil Did It,* and *Victoria's Adventure.*

About the Book

The book is illustrated with pencil drawings.
The text type is set in Bookman and the display
type is set in Bookman and Bookman Demi Italic.